Harriet Can Carry It

By
Kirk Jay Mueller

Illustrated by
Sarah Vonthron-Laver

STAR BRIGHT BOOKS
Cambridge, Massachusetts

Published in the United States of America by Star Bright Books, Inc.
The name Star Bright Books and the Star Bright Books logo are registered trademarks
of Star Bright Books, Inc. Please visit: www.starbrightbooks.com. For bulk orders,
email: orders@starbrightbooks.com, or call customer service at: (617) 354-1300.

Animal Facts by India Futterman

Hardback ISBN-13: 978-1-59572-675-9
Star Bright Books / MA / 00110140
Paperback ISBN-13: 978-1-59572-676-6
Star Bright Books / MA / 00110140

Printed in China (WKT) 10 9 8 7 6 5 4 3 2 1

Printed on paper from sustainable forests and a percentage of post-consumer paper.

To Sierra, Eric, Micah, Jessica, Melissa, Dianne, Joel, Mom, and Dad, with love and best wishes. —KJM

To my lovely girls, Inès and Elise.–S.V.L.

Library of Congress Cataloging-in-Publication Data

Library of Congress Cataloging-in-Publication Data

Mueller, Kirk Jay.
 Harriet can carry it / by Kirk Jay Mueller ; illustrated by Sarah Vonthron-Laver.
    pages cm
 Summary: Harriet, a kangaroo whose job is delivering mail, is worn out and decides
to take her joey to the beach to relax. but along the way, her neighbors ask if she will
carry everything from swim fins to a kayak so they can join her.
 ISBN 978-1-59572-675-9 (hardcover : alk. paper) -- ISBN 978-1-59572-676-6 (pbk.
: alk. paper)
 [1. Stories in rhyme. 2. Letter carriers--Fiction. 3. Kangaroos--Fiction. 4. Animals--
Fiction.] I. Vonthron-Laver, Sarah, illustrator. II. Title.
 PZ8.3.M8678Har 2014
 [E]--dc23
                    2014014178

Harriet Huff had a difficult job.
After working all week, she started to sob,
"A-l-l day l-o-n-g I deliver the mail.
For a strong kangaroo, I'm feeling quite frail.

My poor pouch is worn out from carrying stuff.
I'm sick and I'm tired. Enough is enough!

So I'll take a day off and relax by the sea.
I'll go to the beach where I'll rest and be free."

The next day she awoke. She had a bright plan.
"My Joey and I will leave as soon as we can."

She folded their beach towels right there on the couch,
And placed them so neatly in her giant pouch,
Right next to her Joey, her sweet baby boy,
Along with his Ducky, his favorite toy.

As they left she exclaimed,
"What a beautiful day!"
As she hopped off her porch,
she heard someone yell, **"HEY!"**

It was old Wanda Wombat, so nosey and grouchy,
Asking, "That a beach towel hanging out of your pouchy?
Can I come to the beach? Can I come with YOU?
Will you carry my beach chair? Can I please come too?"

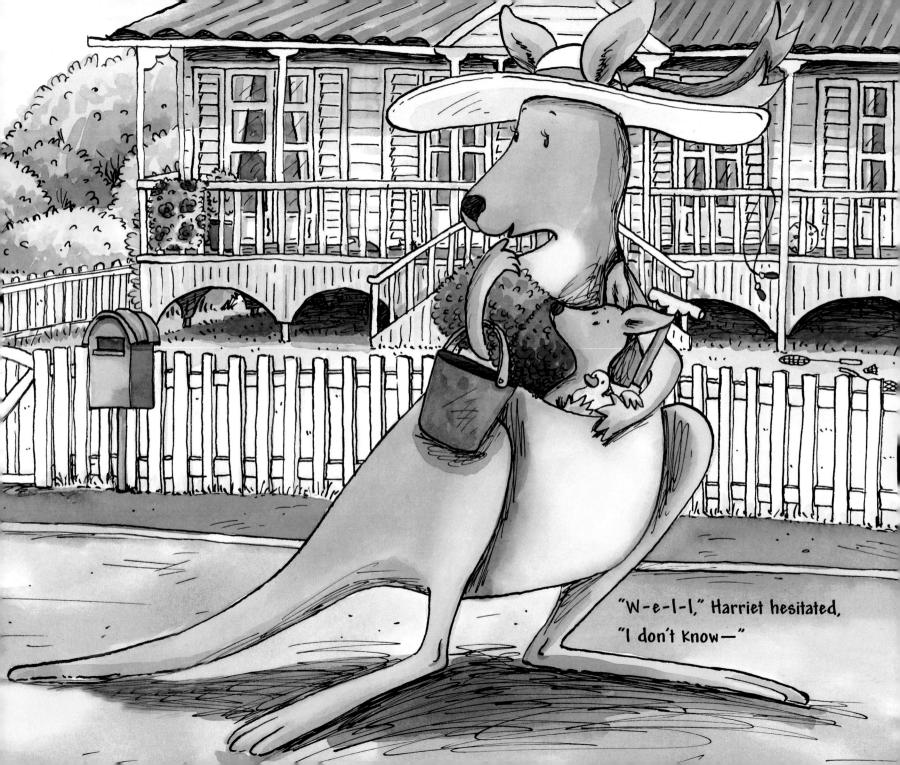

"W-e-l-l," Harriet hesitated,
"I don't know—"

"Of course I can," answered the pushy Wombat.
"You have lots of room. You have loads of space
For tons of stuff in your big pouchy place.
The sun is so bright. The ocean's so blue.
YOU CAN CARRY IT, HARRIET, so I can come too."

Together they trudged up a hill, to the top,
Walked down through a park, when someone yelled, **"STOP!"**

Miss Wallaby Wendy was waiting right there,
With her pink swim-fins on; wind blowing her hair.
"Can I come to the beach? Can I come with YOU?
Will you carry my swim-fins so I can come too?"

"W-e-l-l," Harriet hesitated,
"I'm not sure—"

"Of course you can," answered the bossy Wombat.
"She has lots of room. She has loads of space
For tons of stuff in her big pouchy place.
She is an incredibly kind Kangaroo.
HARRIET CAN CARRY IT, so you can come too."

So on toward the seashore
they walked in a row,
When just past the bike path
someone said, "WHOA!"

BIKE PATH

There stood Kenny Koala, the cool surfer dude,
Who said, "Carry my board, babe." (Which seemed really rude!)
"Can I come to the beach? Can I come with YOU?
Will you carry my surfboard so I can come too?"

"W-e-l-l," Harriet hesitated,
"I don't know—"

"Of course you can," answered the clever Wombat.
"She has lots of room. She has loads of space
For tons of stuff in her big pouchy place.
She's a sensationally strong Kangaroo.
HARRIET CAN CARRY IT, so you can come too."

They'd spotted a palm tree and were jumping for joy,
When off in the distance a voice yelled, "AHOY!"

It was Marcie, the long-tailed marsupial mouse,
Who'd made the mistake of leaving her house
With a huge heavy kayak strapped to her back.
Her long plastic paddle poked out of its sack.
"Can I come to the beach? Can I come with YOU?
Will you carry my kayak so I can come too?"

"W-e-l-l," Harriet hesitated,

"I'm not sure—"

"Of course you can," answered the gutsy Wombat.
"She has lots of room. She has loads of space
For tons of stuff in her big pouchy place.
She is such a graciously good kangaroo.
HARRIET CAN CARRY IT, so you can come too."

Harriet was weary. It was getting late.

As they strolled through the sand dunes, two voices yelled, "WAIT!"

Danny and Dana, the tan Dingo twins,
Were tossing their flying ring around in the wind.
"Can we come to the beach? Can we come with YOU?
Will you carry our flying ring so we can come too?"

"W-e-l-l," Harriet hesitated,

"I don't know—"

"Of course you can," answered Wanda.
"She has lots of room. She has loads of space
For tons of stuff in her big pouchy place.
She is such a naturally nice Kangaroo.
HARRIET CAN CARRY IT, so you can come too."

They all heard some seagulls, smelled salt air and kelp.
When they crossed the road, some guy hollered, **"HELP!"**

Bill Bandicoot was an unpleasant fella
Who was getting quite mad at his bulky umbrella.
"This thing is so heavy I can't even hold it.
Please take it for me, and I'll help you fold it.
Can I come to the beach? Can I come with YOU?
Will you take my umbrella so I can come too?"

"Well," Harriet replied wearily,
"I'm really not sure—"

"M-a-y-b-e... y-o-u pos-sib-ly c-a-n,"
answered Wanda carefully.
"She had lots of room. She had loads of space
For tons of stuff in her big pouchy place.
She looks like a terribly tired kangaroo.
WILL YOU CARRY IT, HARRIET, so he can come too?"

"NO!" Harriet blurted. "ENOUGH IS ENOUGH.
THIS HAS TO STOP. I WON'T CARRY YOUR STUFF!"

Then she threw all their things down into the sand.
Kept her towels and Ducky; took Joey by the hand.
"No way!" she exclaimed while pitching a fit,
"I won't carry your stuff. I just QUIT!"

Just then . . .

Paddy O'Possum was driving along,
Kicking up sand while singing a song.

When they all flagged him down in his stretch pickup truck,
He said, "Pile right in, mates, today you're in luck.
I'm off to the beach and have plenty of room
For you and your stuff, to the seashore we'll zoom."

Harriet picked up her Joey and gave him a hug,
Saying, "Rest in my pouch. You'll be snug as a bug."

With her towels and Joey, plus his yellow Ducky,
They walked to the shore feeling happy-go-lucky.

For she had lots of room. She had loads of space
To carry her boy in her big pouchy place.
Now Harriet felt cheerful, thankful, and calm,
And Joey was happy that she was his mom.

With a gentle breeze blowing and Joey nearby,
Harriet sat on her beach towel and said with a sigh,
"I'll take several days off and relax by the sea.
Just me and my Joey will rest and be free."

Animal Facts

Australia is home to many animals that can't be found in most other places. Evolving on a continent surrounded by water, these creatures developed unique characteristics because they are separated from other climates and species. All of the characters featured in this story, except the dingo, are marsupials, animals that carry their babies in a pouch outside their body. Australia has about 200 species of marsupials!

Kangaroos and Wallabies

You probably know kangaroos by the way they hop – pushing off from their long feet and muscular back legs, which are usually longer than their front limbs. Wallabies are very similar to kangaroos, but they are usually a bit shorter. Both are known as "macropods," which means "big feet." Both kangaroos and wallabies are marsupials and eat mainly grass. Baby kangaroos are called joeys, male kangaroos are called boomers, and female kangaroos are called flyers.

Wombats

These short, stout marsupials may have sharp claws, but they don't use them for hunting. Instead, wombats use these claws to burrow deep into the ground, where they live with several other wombats. Wombats often wander around for hours each night searching for grasses to eat. Highly protective of their feeding grounds, wombats are often aggressive to intruders.

Koalas

Their nickname is "koala bear"; their Latin name (*Phascolarctos cinereus*) means "ash-colored pouched bear" – but koalas aren't bears at all! Koalas spend a lot of their time in eucalyptus trees, whose leaves are their main diet. But since they don't get a lot of energy from the food they eat, koalas spend up to 18 hours a day sleeping!

Marsupial Mice

Although much cuter, marsupial mice are in the same family as the Tasmanian devil! Like the Tasmanian devil, they have sharp teeth, called incisors, for eating insects (and sometimes other animals). While the marsupial mouse might look a lot like the bandicoot, the marsupial mouse is different because it has five separate toes on its back feet, whereas two of the bandicoot's hind toes are attached to each other.

Dingoes

The dingo was introduced to Australia 4,000 years ago by explorers from Asia. At that time, the dingo was domesticated, which meant people kept them as pets. Today, dingoes are considered feral, which means that they became wild after being domesticated at one point. The dingo is the largest carnivorous mammal in Australia. It eats rabbits, mice, and other small animals. The dingo's color allows it to blend in with its desert surroundings, so it can sneak up on its prey.

Bandicoots

These mouse-like marsupials are a common sight in Australian backyards. Bandicoots eat mainly worms, larvae, spiders, and other insects, and they use their long snouts to burrow in the soil for food, often during the night. Bandicoots can be found in many different environments, from rainforests to woodlands, where they build nests, using sticks and leaves.

Possums

You can find possums pretty much everywhere in the world, but the most common possum in Australia is the brush-tailed. They spend the night finding leaves, flowers, and insects to eat, or marking their territory using the smell from special glands on their chests. Possums seek shelter for sleeping during the day, and they often find their way into roofs and ceiling spaces of people's houses.